This book belongs to:

With love to Brooke & Paige...

BLOOMING HEART BOOKS

Getting to the Heart of Complimenting

written by Anne Paluszny
illustrated by Lori McDonough

Starbrook Publishing, Inc. ♥ Carmel, Indiana

To the people who fill my heart with joy...
Mark, A.J., Matthew, Xander and Sarah
-AMP

For my husband, Mark, the hero in my life story,
and for our three main characters...Katelyn, Riley and Griffin
-LCM

A heartfelt thanks to Janet Rodriguez
for being the sunshine that helped this seed to blossom.

Starbrook Publishing, Inc.
484 East Carmel Drive #388, Carmel, Indiana 46032
www.starbrookpublishing.com

The text of this book is set in Minya Nouvelle.
Photography by Stacey Simpson

Printed in Indiana, USA

First Edition

Library of Congress Control Number: 2008910605
ISBN: 978-0-9801958-4-2

♥ A NOTE FROM THE AUTHOR ♥

Welcome to Blooming Heart Books, a series designed to introduce youngsters to the values that "grow" a bigger heart and put them on the path to happiness.

These books are unique - taking readers step-by-step through the process which will allow them to master the life skills that all children should know. No hidden meanings. No morals of the story. No subtle messages to analyze and interpret. Blooming Heart Books get to the heart of each virtue by combining a "how-to" formula with lovable characters and rhyme.

The idea came to me in the midst of raising four little ones. Trying to give a visual for good behavior, I constantly praised them by saying, "Wow, you have a really big heart right now!" It was an easy concept to grasp. Pointing out what made their hearts bloom became a regular game.

It is a dream come true to put words to paper and share these books with you. My heart, right now, is in full bloom.

I wish the same for you...

Anne Paluszny

Gracie   Kat   Simon   Marco   Max   Kimmy

Compliments are kind words
that bring happiness to all.
When you compliment others,
your heart grows big, not small.

Of course,
when compliments come your way,
it's good to know what to do.

So, let's begin today's lesson
with someone complimenting you.

When you receive a compliment,
you should feel special and grand.
Say, "Thank you very much" and smile,
or even shake their hand.

Accept compliments graciously,
each and every day.
Appreciate the kindness
so that more will come your way.

Believe what people tell you...
their kind words are sincere and true.

And since they have just made you feel special...
WOW! Their hearts grew!

Just look into a
person's eyes...

and grin
from ear to ear.

Then share kind
and thoughtful words
that would fill
a heart with cheer.

"What a beautiful dress!"
you say to Mom,
on a very special night.

Then tell Dad
his tie is sharp,
and that it matches
his jacket just right.

A friend will beam as you tell her,
"Wow, your hair is very pretty!"

Let your neighbor know that
his bike is the coolest in the city!

But there's
another way
to compliment,
so before
the day is through,

use kind words
to let others know
that you like
the things
they do.

"Grandpa, I like the way you tell stories about your life as a little boy."

Tell Nana that baking cookies with her is something you really enjoy.

It's true that
compliments like these
are really quite polite.

But it's a
special kind
of compliment
that will make
your heart
shine bright.

Spend time with those you care about,
on the phone if they live far.

Then be sure to mention
that you like them
just for who they are.

There is always something nice to say,

but if you haven't got a clue, just pay attention,
be sincere, and look for something true.

"Uncle Pete, you are so brave!"

Or tell your little brother that he's talented at art.

Maybe tell your cousin that you think he's really funny.

Let your baby sister know
that she's as sweet as honey.

Tell that special someone why they make you feel so proud.

Look into their eyes and grin,
then say it right out loud.

"Nice work!" you say to a classmate.
This will always bring a smile.

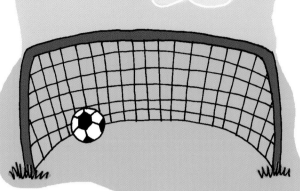

To a teammate say,
"Great shot! You played an awesome game!"

Maybe he will smile at you
and tell you just the same.

MEET THE AUTHOR AND ILLUSTRATOR

Anne Paluszny was born and raised in Ann Arbor, Michigan, but has been a resident of Carmel, Indiana since 1997. She is married to her high-school sweetheart and, together, they are raising four wonderful children. Anne tends to her "blooming heart" each and every day, and is thankful for the many blessings in her life. Visit Anne at www.annepaluszny.com.

Lori McDonough has been doodling ever since she was a little girl and this book is proof that childhood dreams do come true. She lives a whimsical life in Carmel, Indiana with her husband, three fantastic kids and one lovable mutt. They are her joy and inspiration. Visit Lori and her studio at www.lorimcdonough.com.

More Blooming Heart Books are on the way!

Getting to the Heart of Sharing

♥

Getting to the Heart of Respect

♥

Getting to the Heart of Being Responsible

just to name a few...

Visit www.bloomingheartbooks.com for the latest news, as well as fun-filled activities for children.

Miss Josie and the Blooming Heart Bunch

We Give a Round of Applause to

_____

for

Mastering the Art of

Complimenting

and for living life with a

Blooming Heart!

Miss Josie

Miss Josie

_____ Witness

_____ Witness

Date